Alicia Ward-Yarrow - actor, musician, composer and teacher - plays the piano and violin and studied music at Dartington College of Arts in Devon. This was followed by postgraduate studies at Middlesex University. Alicia runs Candeo Dolce, an educational project aimed at promoting confidence, communication skills and social wellbeing among children and young people by using drama, dance and music. She lives in Sunderland and regularly plays in a local northeast orchestra and an Irish ceilidh band.

TWENTY-SIX
Terrifically Terrifying, Twirling, Tantalising, Tiptop, Toe-tapping TONGUE-TWISTERS!

Words and illustrations
by Alicia Ward-Yarrow

Book Guild Publishing
Sussex, England

First published in Great Britain in 2012 by
The Book Guild Ltd
Pavilion View
19 New Road
Brighton, BN1 1UF

Printed and bound in Malaysia under the supervision of
MRM Graphics Ltd, Winslow, Bucks

A catalogue record for this book is available from
The British Library.

ISBN 978 1 84624 733 0

For
Harriet, Eliot,
Thomas and James

A

Agile Agatha the acrobatic alligator

acknowledged the astonished, ambidextrous antelope.

B

The baffled baboon
bounced the balloon

to the badger
playing the bagpipes.

The camel
with the
collywobbles
carried the
custard
carefully,

but crashed into
the clever clown,
clattering his castanets!

D

The dancing daisies
dazzled the dizzy dandelions.

Eliza the elegant and
effervescent elephant

liked to examine
the exciting encyclopaedia.

F

Forty-five flowery fairies danced the fancy foxtrot

to the fast
and flashy,
flowing music
of the fabulous,
fascinating fiddle.

'The greedy, grumpy goat gobbled the grass in the garden,'

gabbled the giggling girl as she gaped at the glittering galaxy.

H

Hector the
happy, hiccupping
hedgehog

hurried to help Harry
the hula-hooping hippopotamus.

I see indigo icicles
inside the igloo

where the indulgent iguana
has his eye on the ice cream.

L

The little, lucky ladybird
left a little, lemon lollipop

for the lively, laughing lamb
who lolloped along the lane.

The mischievous monkey
merrily muttered to the
magnificent magician
making meringues:

'We
must
march
many
miles
to the
mysterious maze
to marvel at the melodious music.'

N

Never go near the
notorious nettle –

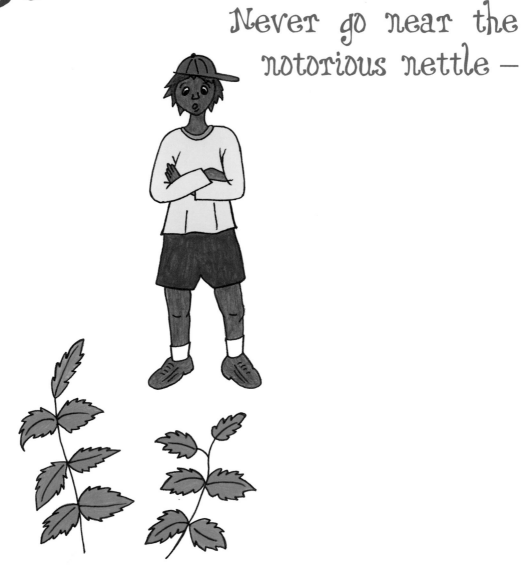

it's nasty

and nothing
but a nuisance.

Octavia the octopus
was often optimistic
and objected to every obstacle
that obstructed the orchestra,

but the otter and the ostrich
were outrageously outspoken
and the outburst that they offered
was just obviously too obnoxious!

P

The panther popped the ping-pong
as he passed the precious parcel
to the pleasant panda playing
a polka upon the piano.

There was quarrelling and quibbling, quivering and quaking,

as the quality of the quiche did not qualify to serve the Queen.

'It's rock 'n' roll!'
raved the rocking radio
with a rondo rhythm
and a rattling reel!

The rhinoceros raced,
the rabbit ran
to the roly-poly rhapsody
at Rendezvous Road!

'The skipping squirrel squabbled at the scarecrow's secret scherzo,'

sang the swishing, swooping, sweeping swan, serenely singing a song.

T

The tiny, talented,
tartan teddy
got tangled in the tango,

tapped on the tambourine
and trotted on the trampoline.

The table toppled,
the trifle trickled,
the tutti-frutti tripled
and the treacle toffee tickled.

There were
umpteen umpires
unaware of the unicorn,

underneath the umbrella
in his unique uniform.

The viola and the violin
have very vivacious voices.
The vital volume of these virtuosos
is varied, valued and vivid.

The weary walrus waltzed,
whilst whistling wonderfully well.

Whoops!

... After a whirl he wobbled!

Whoopee!

... After a wobble he whirled!

Exuberant Xenia,
though exhausted and exasperated,
expertly excelled
on the exhilarating xylophone.

Y

You
yo-yoed
your
yo-yo
then yelled
'Yahoo!'
After a yarn you yawned
then yodelled and yelped.

Z

The zebra was so zealous
that he zoomed in a zigzag zone.

Then he zipped
down to zero
to play his zither
with zest at the zoo.